The Reader

by Amy Hest • *illustrated by* Lauren Castillo

Amazon Children's Publishing

For Emma, with love
—A.H.

For Kurt, an inspirational illustrator,
mentor, and friend
—L.C.

Amazon Publishing
Attn: Amazon Children's Books
P.O. Box 400818
Las Vegas, NV 89149
www.amazon.com/amazonchildrenspublishing

Library of Congress Cataloging-in-Publication Data

Hest, Amy.
The reader / by Amy Hest ; illustrated by Lauren Castillo. — 1st ed.
p. cm.
Summary: A boy and his dog hike to the top of a very tall, snowy hill
where they play, enjoy a snack, and then share their favorite book before
sledding home.
ISBN 978-0-7614-6184-5 (hardcover) — ISBN 978-0-7614-6185-2 (ebook)
[1. Snow—Fiction. 2. Books and reading—Fiction. 3. Dogs—Fiction.] I.
Castillo, Lauren, ill. II. Title.
PZ7.H4375Rdm 2012
[E]—dc23
2011046914

The illustrations are rendered in ink and watercolor.
Book design by Anahid Hamparian
Editor: Melanie Kroupa

Printed in China (W)
First edition
10 9 8 7 6 5 4 3 2 1

Amazon Children's Publishing

The reader has a small brown dog
and a sturdy suitcase that is brown . . .

and a long red sled with a long, loopy rope
for pulling through deep snow.

His boots are high and very heavy, but he is strong, and his train tracks are impeccably straight. They are beautiful.

The dog skips off, a bouncing dot, chasing his tail . . .
a bunny . . . a blue jay . . . his tail.

Then off he goes to the top of the hill to wait.

He is good at waiting.

The reader comes slowly,
pulling his sled across the world.
It is hard work, but he is good at working hard.

The wind blows. Snow blows.

The hill is very, very tall.

The top is far, far away.

Up and up he climbs,
tilting in the wind,
pulling in the blowing snow.

And then he is there, at the top of the world.

"Here I am!" says the reader to the dog.

They make angels . . .
snowballs . . . more angels . . .

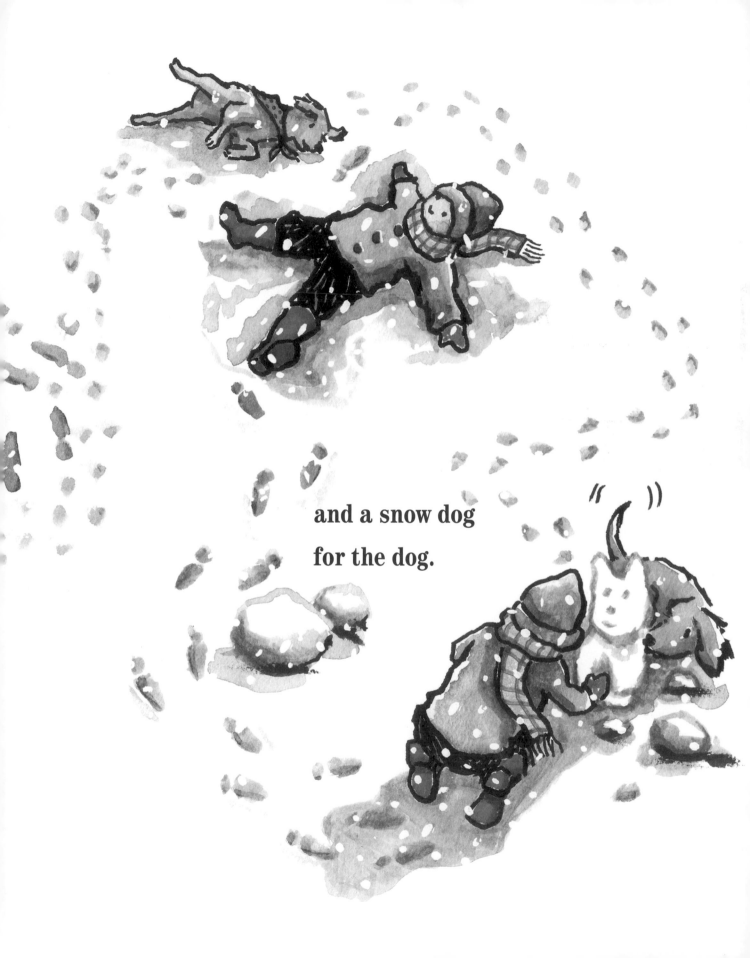

and a snow dog
for the dog.

It is shivery-cold at the top of the world.

But there are warm drinks and crunchy toast for two.

Snow falls.

And the only sound in the world is

sssip-crunch-crunch . . . sssip-crunch-crunch.

When there is nothing left to crunch or sip,
they curl up close.

"And now," says the reader to the dog, "it's time."

Slowly, he opens the suitcase.

Click. Click.

A book. The very best book.

"*Two Good Friends*," says the reader to the dog,

and he opens the book to the very first page.

The dog waits. It is hard, but he is good at waiting.

And then at last the reader reads.

And the only sound in the world is
the sound of the reader reading
to the very last page . . .
the very last word.

*"**Two Good Friends,**"* says the reader to the dog.

"Just like us!"

The dog licks his nose.

They pack up the suitcase.

Click. Click.

Then the reader wraps the dog in his two strong arms.

And off they go!

Fast . . . and faster still
to the bottom of the hill . . .

across the world . . .

And then they are there.

Home. Together.